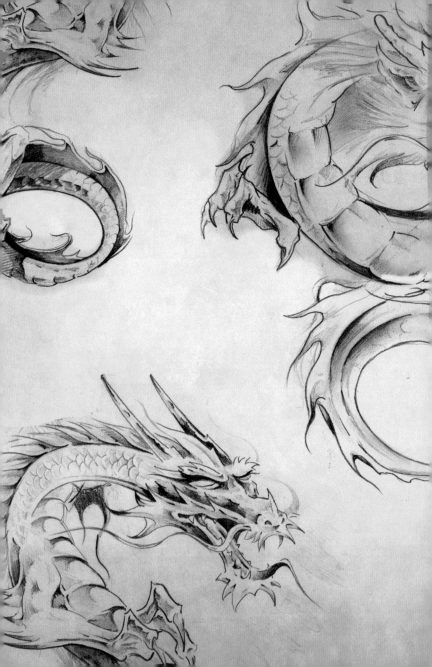

DRAGONBORN

The Dragon with the Girl Tattoo

BY MICHAEL DAHL

ILLUSTRATED BY LUIGI AIME

STONE ARCH
BOOKS™

ZONE BOOKS ARE PUBLISHED BY
STONE ARCH BOOKS
A CAPSTONE IMPRINT
1710 ROE CREST DRIVE
NORTH MANKATO, MINNESOTA 56003
WWW.CAPSTONEPUB.COM

LIBRARY OF CONGRESS CATALOGING-IN-PUBLICATION DATA
DAHL, MICHAEL.
THE DRAGON WITH THE GIRL TATTOO / WRITTEN BY MICHAEL DAHL ; ILLUSTRATED BY LUIGI AIME.
P. CM. -- [DRAGONBORN]

SUMMARY: A STRANGE NEW KID AT SCHOOL HAS A WEIRD TATTOO ON HIS ARM. IS IT A PICTURE
OF THE SCHOOL'S MOST POPULAR GIRL? SHE IGNORES THE LONER UNTIL SHE FINDS HERSELF IN A
DANGEROUS SITUATION WHERE ONLY THE BOY'S MYSTERIOUS SECRET CAN SAVE HER.

ISBN: 978-1-4342-4041-5 [LIBRARY BINDING]
ISBN: 978-1-4342-4257-0 [PBK.]
ISBN 978-1-4342-4625-7 [EBOOK]
1. DRAGONS--JUVENILE FICTION. 2. FRIENDSHIP--JUVENILE FICTION. [1. DRAGONS--FICTION. 2.
FRIENDSHIP--FICTION.] I. AIME, LUIGI, ILL. II. TITLE.
PZ7.D15134OV 2012
813.54--DC23   2012004508

ART DIRECTOR: KAY FRASER
GRAPHIC DESIGNER: HILARY WACHOLZ
PRODUCTION SPECIALIST: KATHY MCCOLLEY

PHOTO CREDITS:
SHUTTERSTOCK: CAESART [METAL PLATE, PP. 1, 4, 66]; FERNANDO CORTES [DRAGON PATTERN]

PRINTED IN THE UNITED STATES OF AMERICA AT CORPORATE GRAPHICS
IN NORTH MANKATO, MINNESOTA.
102012   007006R

TABLE OF CONTENTS

A NEW AGE OF DRAGONS HAS BEGUN.

DRAGONBORN

Young people around the world have discovered that dragon blood flows in their veins. They are filled with new power and new ideas. But before they reveal themselves to the world, they must find one another . . .

CHAPTER 1
Loser

A dark-haired boy sat alone at a table in the school cafeteria.

He ate his lunch, staring out the windows.

Behind him, the other students laughed and yelled and chattered.

The boy didn't hear them. All he could think about was the sky.

A blue sky full of gigantic clouds and swirls of dead leaves.

Inside the cafeteria, two girls got up from a nearby table.

They walked over to the kitchen window to return their trays.

One of the girls elbowed her friend and giggled. She pointed at the dark-haired boy sitting alone. "That's Weird Andy," said the girl. "The new guy. Have you seen his tattoo?"

Her friend shook her head.

"Take a look, but don't say anything," whispered the first girl.

They quickly glanced at the boy's arm as they walked past his table.

A tattoo covered his right arm. It looked like a smiling girl with short blond hair.

On his other arm was a birthmark, shaped like a dragon.

The two marks seemed to balance each other.

It was as if the boy had gotten the tattoo so that people wouldn't stare at the birthmark.

The second girl gasped. "It looks exactly like Lizzie!" she said. "Does Lizzie know about this?"

The first girl shook her head.

"That's creepy," the second girl said. Then she added, "Let's go find her!"

The two friends hurried over to another table. A blond girl with a wide smile was laughing with her friends. She was just getting up from the table, ready to leave.

The two girls stopped her. "Have you seen it?" one of them asked Lizzie.

All three girls stared over at Andy. Lizzie frowned and rolled her eyes. "Yeah, yeah," she said. "I've seen it."

"He likes you, Lizzie," said one of her friends.

"Well, I don't like him," said Lizzie.

She picked up her books from the table.

"He's a loser," she added, and walked away.

CHAPTER 2
Unfair Fight

Andy moved his arm and covered his tattoo. He had seen the girls laughing at him.

He knew they were talking about him. Without thinking, he patted his right arm.

The tattoo was more important to him than the girls realized.

Andy saw the blond girl pick up her books and walk away.

If they only knew, he thought.

Andy stood up quickly from his table and stared outside.

A noise had startled him.

It was a noise no other students could hear through the thick walls of concrete and glass.

It echoed from the far side of the school, behind the tall, blank walls of the gym.

The noise was a desperate cry.

Andy found a door leading outside.

He ran across the schoolyard, following the noise.

Andy had heard the sound many times before. Usually, he was the one making it.

"Stop!" someone was yelling.

A thin boy named Vik was kneeling on the ground.

Blood covered his face from a gash on his cheek. One eye was swollen shut.

His shirt was ripped, the sign of a recent fight.

Vik stared at the ground, but he still cried out. "It's . . . too much! Stop."

Five boys surrounded Vik.

They stood in the shadows of the high gym walls.

One of them darted up to Vik and kicked him in the side. Then he quickly ran back to join his friends.

The boys in the circle all laughed.

Vik fell to the ground. He groaned and coughed into the dirt.

Andy took a step forward. "What's going on?" he asked.

A tall, strong boy named Garrett stepped out of the shadows. "None of your business," he answered.

"Weird Andy," mocked one of Garrett's buddies.

Garrett looked hard at Andy. "Get out of here," Garrett said. "Or you're next."

"I don't think so," said Andy.

Vik, still lying on the ground, waved a weak hand at Andy.

"It's not worth it," Vik said, gasping. "Just . . . just go."

CHAPTER 3
Unfair Winds

Garrett stopped smiling.

A gigantic cloud suddenly darkened the sky.

Cold winds blew around the gym building.

Gusts whistled and screamed,
drowning out the boys' mean laughter.

The shadows grew wide.

The darkness deepened.

Dead leaves and dirt whirled around
the circle of boys.

"What's that?" one of them yelled. He pointed to a shadow next to the wall.

The shadow lifted its head and roared.

Two monstrous wings reached out toward the boys.

Sharp claws flexed open and shut.

On one of the creature's scaly arms was a small patch of brightness.

There, the scales seemed to make a shape.

The shape was of a girl with blond hair.

The creature roared again.

The boys screamed and ran.

Moments later, the winds grew weaker.

The gigantic cloud overhead turned into smaller and smaller pieces.

Garrett and the others were gone.

Only Vik was left. And Andy.

"What happened?" asked Vik, his face angry and bloody.

"It's Vik, right?" asked Andy. He held out his hand and helped the other boy stand up.

Vik nodded. "I'm okay," he said. "You're Weird — I mean, you're Andy, right?"

"Yeah," said Andy.

Vik looked around. "I don't get it. Where did they go?" he asked.

Andy smiled. "It was an unfair fight," he said. He rubbed the birthmark on his left arm. The one shaped like a dragon. He added, "I guess they figured that out and left."

"You should have left too," said Vik.

He wiped his bloody nose on his sleeve. Then he turned and, without looking back at Andy, he quickly walked away.

Andy stared after him. "You're welcome," he said to the empty air.

CHAPTER 4
Ambush

Andy had stayed late at school. Now it was dark as he hurried home.

A night wind whipped through the alleys and narrow streets.

Andy turned up the collar of his leather jacket.

He shoved his hands into the pockets. The jacket felt warm against the cold wind.

The jacket also covered up the rip in his shirt where the two dragon wings had sprouted.

Andy was thinking about how strangely Vik had acted.

He was thinking about the girl named Lizzie.

He remembered her friends laughing and staring at him in the cafeteria.

Andy couldn't wait to get home.

As he thought about the day, Andy remembered the sound of Vik's voice.

It had sounded so desperate.

There it is again, he thought. *Vik's voice.*

It was coming from the nearby alley. "Help!"

Andy frowned. *Are they after him again?* he wondered.

He stepped into the dark alley. Vik's cry was coming from around the far corner.

Seconds later, Andy was at the end of the alley.

Vik was standing with his back against the wall.

"Vik!" yelled Andy.

"Andy," said Vik. "You came."

His face was still bruised. His one eyes still swollen shut. "I was hoping you would," he added, calmly.

Andy frowned. "What's going on?" he asked. "I thought someone was hurting you."

Vik shook his head. "No one's hurting me," he said. "I'm just here with my friends."

Two figures walked out from the shadows behind Andy.

They grabbed him with powerful hands.

They pulled off his jacket and flung it into the dirt, and then forced his arms behind his back.

Andy looked at his captors.

One of them was Garrett.

"These are my new friends," Vik said. We were just having a little initiation when you butted in earlier."

Garrett chuckled. "But the initiation's not over," he said. "You're part of it now, freak!"

Andy looked into Vik's eyes. "They beat you up," Andy said.

Vik was quiet.

Garrett wrenched Andy's arm behind his back. He said, "We just wanted to see how much Vik could take. Before we let him be part of our team."

"What kind of team is that?" asked Andy.

Garrett's eyes glowed dull bronze. The irises were shaped like a lizard's. No one else could see his eyes except Andy.

"I think you know," Garrett whispered.

Vik stepped closer to Andy and said, "Now let's see how much you can take."

He smiled and slugged Andy in the stomach.

CHAPTER 5
The Call of the Tattoo

Andy groaned and let out a gasp of air.

His body doubled up in pain.

He grunted from each new punch.

The boys tightened their grip on his arms as he struggled to break free.

Another voice tore through the darkness of the alley. A girl's voice.

"Stop it!" she called. Footsteps rushed into the alley. Andy forced open his eyes and saw Lizzie.

A neon billboard somewhere high above them shone down on her bright hair.

It almost hurt him to look at her.

"Stop it!" she repeated. "Leave him alone. Three against one! You call that fair?"

The boys let go of Andy.

He collapsed onto the dirty floor of the alley.

Lizzie stared at the three standing boys.

"Why can't you leave people alone?" she cried.

"What's he? Your boyfriend?" said Garrett.

"Yeah, right," said Lizzie. "He doesn't have to be my boyfriend just because I want you to stop hurting him."

Andy groaned.

"So you don't have a boyfriend?" asked Garrett. "What about me?"

"What about you?" said Lizzie with a sneer.

She turned and started back down the alley. The boys followed her.

Andy was barely awake, but he heard Lizzie scream.

The dragon tattoo on his arm began to burn. The warmth traveled upward and eased his wrenched shoulders. It flowed down into his stomach and melted the pain.

Andy looked at his other arm, at the other tattoo.

It glowed like gold.

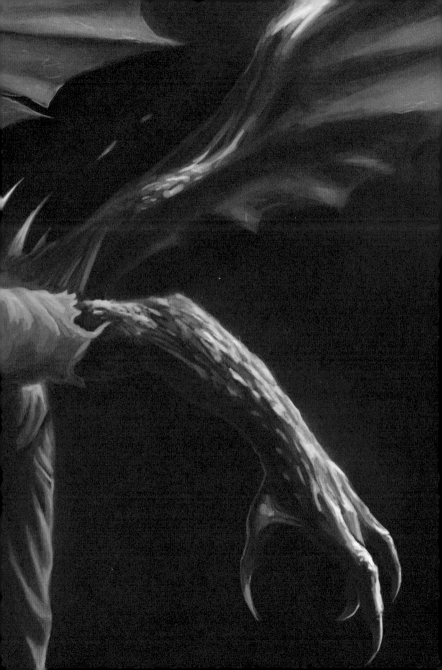

CHAPTER 4
Dangerous

Andy shouted to Lizzie, but the shout turned into a roar. Garrett and the others looked back. Andy was gone.

In his place was a monstrous creature with leathery wings. Its wings scraped against the brick walls of the alley.

The creature's eyes burned in the darkness. "Run!" screamed Vik.

The boys let go of Lizzie and rushed toward the alley's entrance.

A shower of flame shot past their heads. Two huge claws lunged out of the darkness.

The dragon seized the running boys in its deadly talons. Garrett fought against the fierce grip. He could barely breathe.

The other boys were squeezed together in the other claw.

Without warning, the creature soared into the air.

Lizzie screamed again, but the sound soon died away.

The boys were high above the city. Their feet dangled helplessly over the roofs of buildings and swaying power lines.

Then the dragon's blazing eyes spied the river far below. The boys saw it too.

"No! No!" cried Vik.

The creature let go of Garrett. He dove into the mist.

Soon, a shadowy serpent twisted and flew through the night.

The creature that had been Garrett roared. It sounded almost like laughter.

CHAPTER 7
The Girl on His Arm

Lizzie stood alone in the alley.

She looked up and saw a shape like a monstrous crow. It flew past her head and disappeared into the shadows.

A moment later, she heard footsteps.

It was Andy.

Lizzie's eyes grew wide with fear.

"Don't worry," he said. "They're on the roof of a building far from here. They'll find a way to get down."

He thought of how Garrett had flown away in fear.

He thought of a pair of sickly green wings.

"And please," said Andy. "Don't tell anyone what happened."

"Don't worry," she said. Then Lizzie chuckled lightly. "Even if I did, no one would believe me."

Andy was holding his jacket in his hand. His bare arms were exposed to the cold.

Lizzie looked at the tattoo. "Who is that?" she asked.

Without thinking, Andy reached for the tattoo. He patted it gently.

"This is my sister," he said, not looking at it. "She and my brother and I all lived together. Used to live together, I mean. She died last year."

"I'm sorry," said Lizzie. She looked at it closely. "My friends," she said. "They're silly. They thought it was me."

Andy looked down at the figure of the happy blond girl and smiled. "Yeah," he said. "It could be you."

Lizzie smiled back. Then she said, "She's pretty."

"Yes," said Andy. He stared hard at Lizzie.

Lizzie shivered a little. "It's cold," she said.

Andy helped her put on the jacket.

He noticed a small birthmark on the back of her neck.

It looked like a dragon's tail.

"I think I need to get home," said Lizzie.

"Me too," Andy said.

They passed through the alley, and together they walked out to the street.

AUTHOR

Michael Dahl is the author of more than 200 books for children and young adults. He has won the AEP Distinguished Achievement Award three times for his nonfiction. His Finnegan Zwake mystery series was shortlisted twice by the Anthony and Agatha awards. He has also written the Dragonblood series. He is a featured speaker at conferences around the country on graphic novels and high-interest books for boys.

ILLUSTRATOR

Luigi Aime was born in 1987 in Savigliano, a small Italian city near Turin. Even when he was only three years old, he loved to draw. He attended art school, graduating with honors in Illustration and Animation from the European Institute of Design in Milan, Italy.

DISCUSSION QUESTIONS

1. Which of the characters in this book have dragon blood?

2. Why do Vik and the other boys attack Andy?

3. What questions do you still have about this story? Discuss them!

WRITING PROMPTS

1. Write a short story about Andy's sister. What do you think she was like?

2. It can be very interesting to think about a story from another person's point of view. Try writing this story, or part of it, from Lizzie's point of view. What does she see, hear, think, and say? What does she notice? How is the story different?

3. Create a cover for a book. It can be this book or another book you like, or a made-up book. Don't forget to write the information on the back, and include the author and illustrator names!

GLOSSARY

ambush (AM-bush)—to hide and then attack someone

birthmark (BURTH-mark)—a mark on the skin that was there from birth

desperate (DESS-pur-it)—in need of help

exposed (ek-SPOZED)—uncovered

gigantic (jye-GAN-tik)—huge, or enormous

initiation (i-nish-ee-AY-shuhn)—a ceremony that brings someone into a group

mocked (MOKD)—made fun of

monstrous (MON-struhss)—huge, frightening

sickly (SIK-lee)—seeming ill or weak

tattoo (ta-TOO)—a picture that has been printed onto someone's skin

unfair (uhn-FAIR)—not fair, right, or just

THEY MUST WORK TOGETHER TO
FIGHT THE COMING BATTLE. BUT FIRST
THEY MUST FIND EACH OTHER ...

ANDY HARRIS

When Andy was little, his older brother liked to jump out from behind doors and scare him. When Andy was eight, his brother scared him and Andy's eyes turned orange. He said it looked like Andy had snake eyes. He said Andy looked taller, too. After that, he never scared Andy again.

Age: 15
Hometown: Santa Rosa, California
Dragon appearance: Green and magenta
Dragon species: *Draconis patronis* ("defending dragon")
Strength: Protection